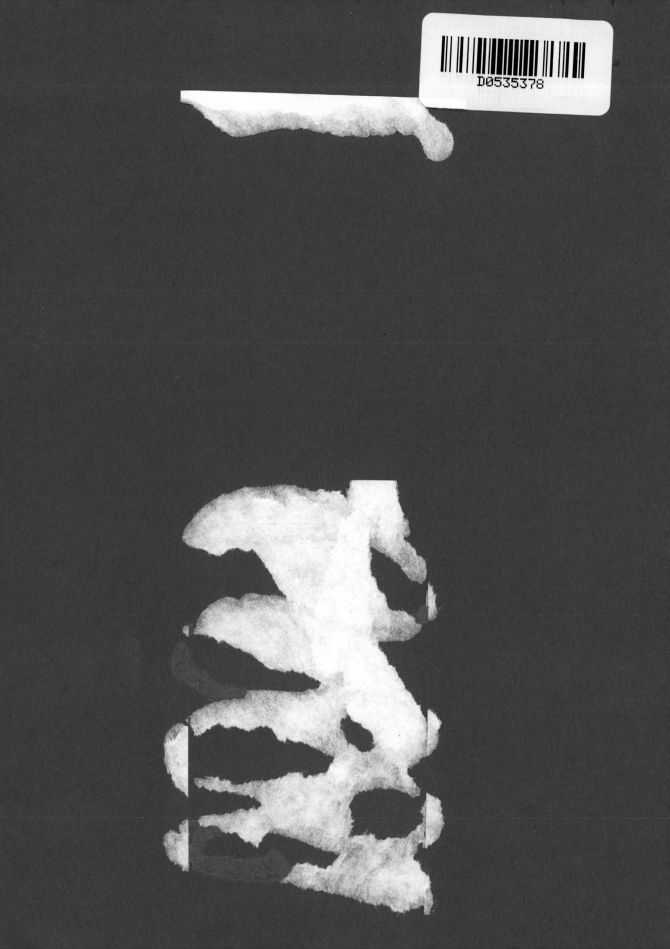

THE ORPHELINES
IN THE
ENCHANTED CASTLE

THE ORPHELINES
IN THE
ENCHANTED CASTLE

BY

Natalie Savage Carlson

PICTURES BY

Adriana Saviozzi

HARPER & ROW, PUBLISHERS
NEW YORK, EVANSTON, AND LONDON

THE ORPHELINES IN THE ENCHANTED CASTLE

Text copyright © 1964 by Natalie Savage Carlson
Pictures copyright © 1964 by Adriana Saviozzi

Library of Congress catalog card number: 63-14368

FOR SISTER EVANGELINE

THE ORPHELINES
IN THE
ENCHANTED CASTLE

CHAPTER ONE

Once upon a time there were twenty beautiful French princesses who were going to live in an enchanted castle with their fairy godmother and their thirty knights.

The princesses were really the twenty little *orphelines*, as the French call girl orphans, and their fairy godmother was plump, kindly Madame Flattot, the woman in charge of them. The noble knights were the thirty boy orphans who would share the castle with them.

And the castle was to be their new orphanage. It was in the forest of Fontainebleau, south of Paris, waiting for them to bring it to life again—as the prince had done in THE SLEEPING BEAUTY OF THE WOODS.

"Of course the castle will be enchanted," Madame Flattot assured the girls. "Everyone knows that the forest of Fontainebleau is full of fairies and witches. And the ghostly huntsman who rides with his pack of dogs."

Genevieve, the young girl who helped take care of the children, rolled her blue eyes fearfully. "There is a robbers' cave there," she stated, "and my godmother said that there are wolves in the forest."

"Bah!" scoffed Madame. "Who cares for wolves?" She tossed her false braid and lifted a corner of her apron. "In the forest of Fontainebleau even *I* shall be enchanting," she declared.

She danced a few steps of the stately minuet and ended with a deep curtsey to the moving man who was also bowing to her because he was carrying out a table on his back.

But, alas! The move to the enchanted castle was poorly timed. It came on St. Médard's Day, when it is said that even one drop of rain foretells forty days of wet weather.

St. Médard is the good saint who, in medieval times, answered the prayers of drought-stricken farmers, and he has never learned that one can get too much of his rain.

The long trip to the castle was made in a downpour, so the disappointed orphelines could see only a blur of green leaves and black tree trunks as they drove through the famous forest.

Madame Flattot sat in back of the autobus with Coucky on her lap. He was the little Arab baby who had been abandoned in the bread basket of the girls' orphanage. For a long anxious time it had looked as if he would be taken away from the girls and put in the boys'

2

orphanage. But now that both orphanages were to be combined, the orphelines did not have to worry about losing their littlest brother. And they could hardly wait to meet their thirty new brothers.

The girls squeezed against the windows. Genevieve wiped a round spot free of moisture on her pane and searched the great tree trunks and piles of gray rocks for the forms of fleeing wolves.

"I saw something running over the rocks that might have been a big dog," she said. "It really could have been a dog. Maybe it *was* a dog."

"I think it was a wolf," said Brigitte, tossing back her thick braid that was like a tassel of millet seeds. "And if you weren't in this autobus, you could be Little Red Hood and talk to him about your godmother."

She was the happiest orpheline and the first one to think of a new game or remember an old story.

Yvette, who was near Brigitte's age, tried to still Genevieve's fears. "If a wolf ever comes near you," she said, "our thirty knights will protect you. They will slay the wolf." Of course, Coucky wasn't old enough even to slay a beetle so they could not count him among their knights yet.

"I will be satisfied with the knights if they are obedient boys with clean faces and polite habits," said Genevieve. "I won't expect them to kill wolves."

4

"Perhaps the wolves will chase our cats," worried curly haired Josine, the youngest. She was worried about the ten cats the orphelines had adopted at a cat show in Paris.

"Do not worry about the cats," said Genevieve. "They have been sent to the castle's farm already, so they can live happily ever after in the barn."

Madame Flattot, with Coucky still in her arms, went forward to consult the driver of the autobus. She came back beaming.

"He says we are getting close to the castle now," she told the children. "First we will come to the village." She wiped the window with her handkerchief. "Oh, that St. Médard and his rain!" she exclaimed. "But in three days it will be St. Barnabé's Day, and if the sun shines even a minute, St. Médard's nose will be cut and we shall have good weather from then on through the summer."

"Will St. Médard's nose really be cut?" asked Yvette in a shocked voice.

"Of course not," replied Madame. "It is only the old-time way of saying that St. Barnabé will turn off St. Médard's rain."

The driver's information was correct because the road went out of the trees and wound through the narrow street of a village. It curled around the village square with its rusty statue of a World War I soldier and past the church whose steeple was crumbling with age.

Then back into the trees went the autobus and in two jerks and a backfire they drew up to the castle.

It was small as castles are measured, and certainly nothing to compare with the royal palace of Fontaine-bleau, but it really looked as if it belonged in a fairy tale. On one side of the entrance was a squat round donjon with flat top and on the other a graceful pointed tower, like a saltshaker and pepper pot set precisely against a fluted soup tureen. A real moat circled the building, but in place of a drawbridge was a sturdy concrete bridge that led to the recessed entrance.

The orphelines clasped their hands and sighed with blissful delight, but Madame Flattot was not so charmed. "Oh, là!" she cried. "They haven't filled the moat yet. And already water is gathering in it from the rain."

"I will have to keep my third eye on the girls all the time," said Genevieve, because she feared drownings even more than wolves.

Madame Flattot had one consolation. "At least I have been assured that the furniture has arrived and been put in place," she comforted herself. "And Monsieur de Goupil told me that there are fine new desks in the classrooms—although that will be of no use to us now that it is summer vacation."

Monsieur de Goupil was the head of both orphanages so he had to think of everything. He had even thought of buying his brother-in-law's old deserted castle so the boys and girls could live together in one big family.

"I do hope my portrait of Napoleon wasn't damaged in the moving," fretted Madame, "that is, no more than it was when I bought it." She had purchased the oil painting at the Ham and Iron Fair in Paris, dickering with the dealer until he had lowered his price for the last time.

The painting had since hung in the place of honor in the orphanage parlor.

But the girls weren't interested in the furniture or Napoleon's picture.

"Have the boys come yet?" one of them asked as they rose from their seats and crowded the aisle. "Did our knights get here ahead of us?"

"I don't think so," said Madame as the autobus came to a stop by the footbridge. "Now don't worry about the boys. Worry about the rain. When the door is opened, everyone run for the castle as fast as possible. Pretend that Genevieve's wolves are chasing you and safety lies within the castle."

So, as soon as the door of the bus opened, the orphelines screamed shrilly and ran to the recessed door.
And to hasten them even more, Genevieve ran behind
them making growling noises.

When they entered the great hall, they fell silent with
awe. There was an enormous fireplace at each end and
over the stairway was mounted the head of a stag. To
be sure, part of an antler had been broken off and the
hair had been eaten by a century of moths, but he still
served as a reminder that this had been one of the old
hunting castles of the forest of Fontainebleau.

"Where's the rest of him?" asked Josine, because she

8

thought that the stag had thrust his head through the wall.

She promptly went running up the stone steps to find the room behind the stag's head which should contain his body.

Madame Flattot admired the great fireplaces. "It will be such a problem to decide over which one to hang Napoleon's portrait." She sighed. "Now would he prefer to look at the stag or would he have better light by the windows at the other end? I think he would do better in the light. But I am overlooking the most important thing. I must see the kitchen. Monsieur tells me that everything is new. There is even a modern gas stove." She saluted the spot where Napoleon's picture would hang. "You had your empire and I have mine," she announced to the picture that hadn't been hung yet. "My kingdom is my kitchen."

The kitchen was almost as large as the great hall and as dark. But a shiny chrome sink had been added to one corner and close to it was a new stove that gleamed silver and white. Over it hung rows and rows of bright new metal pots and pans.

Madame lifted a pan from its peg critically. She juggled it disapprovingly.

"Regard my battery of cooking pots," she said to

Genevieve. "Would Napoleon have sent his troops into battle with tin cannons?" She held the pot at arm's length. "It does not even bend my wrist," she complained. "It should be of iron or copper and almost too heavy to lift. And this omelette pan next to it. If I cooked eggs in this thin pan, the whites would burn or turn to rubber. I shall insist to Monsieur de Goupil that I get my old iron pots back."

"But these pans look so pretty hanging on the wall over the stove," said Genevieve. "And they make the castle more modern."

"I may live in a modern castle," pronounced Madame Flattot, "but I am an old-fashioned cook. That is why I can make cheap food taste so good."

She looked into the oven. She tried to light one of the burners. Nothing happened. She looked behind the stove.

"*Hélas*, Genevieve," she mourned, "we do not live in a modern castle yet. The stove is not connected. Now how can I get supper?"

The orphelines loved the discovery that the new-fashioned stove was not connected.

"The big fireplaces, Madame," cried Brigitte. "Since you are an old-fashioned cook, you can cook in one of them. It will be like the olden times in the castle."

10

"And where will the wood for the fireplace come from?" asked Madame. "Do you think we are living in one of your fairy tales where hands with invisible bodies will carry in logs for the fireplace and lay the cloth for a feast?"

It really seemed like living in a fairy tale because no sooner had Madame said these magic words than invisible hands began pounding on the heavy outer door.

"It's the boys," cried Brigitte excitedly. "The boys have arrived. They can look for some wood."

But it was not the boys. It was a man in dripping blue work clothes and muddy wooden shoes. Clinging to his hand was Josine. She was smeared with mud from her curly hair to her soaking shoes.

"I came to bring you the message that the boys will not arrive until after supper," explained the man. "Then I found this little one caught in the moat. I'm Hubert, one of the farm workers," he added hastily.

Madame Flattot was aghast. The orphelines opened their mouths in astonishment. The last time they had seen Josine she was running up the stairs to find the room behind the stag.

"I couldn't find the rest of the stag," said Josine, "so I looked out of the window and I saw a little snake in

11

the moat. I didn't want him to drown so I found a back door and went out to save him."

"A snake!" shrieked Madame Flattot. "You tried to catch a snake?"

Hubert handed Josine to her. "It was only a harmless water snake," he explained, "and the water in the moat isn't deep enough to drown a child. But the sides were so slippery that she couldn't get out."

Madame Flattot began to marshal her forces after the first shock.

"Take her upstairs and try to find a bathroom," she said to Genevieve. "And pray that the water pipes are connected. If they are, give her a good hot bath. And if there is no hot water, give her a brisk rubbing down after you have washed off the mud. And if there is no water, we will have to set pots out in the rain to catch some. Those new ones should be good for that."

Then like the good general she was, Madame Flattot turned the disaster into victory. "Can you please bring us some wood, Hubert?" she asked the farm worker. "And build a roaring fire in the fireplace under Napoleon's picture."

Genevieve and Hubert quickly obeyed Madame's orders, although the farmer had to be shown which of the fireplaces was to be under Napoleon's picture.

12

Madame Flattot caught her breath and shook her finger at the orphelines. "And don't anyone dare go outside until the rain stops and the moat is dry," she commanded.

Hubert's wooden shoes clacked back and forth over the stone floors, leaving a trail of muddy footprints. Madame brought a mop from the kitchen and followed behind him as he carried in load after load of fire logs.

The orphelines were disappointed that the boys would not arrive for supper. But it was fun to watch Madame bustling around the fireplace like a cook of old. She filled the biggest pot she could find with the meat and vegetables she had had the foresight to bring along with them.

Soon a delicious smell was coming from the fireplace. The great logs crackled and the flames leaped higher and higher. Black soot gathered on the sides of the big pot. Madame's face grew redder and redder from the heat of the fire.

"It may not be breast of white peacock," she apologized, "but it will taste as good."

Then she ladled her stew into bowls she found in a cupboard and gave the children big spoons from a drawer. The orphelines and Coucky squatted on the stone floor with their bowls and didn't have to mind

13

their table manners. It was such a wonderful feast in the enchanted castle. They only regretted that the boys couldn't have shared the meal with them.

After they had carried out their dirty dishes and spoons, the orphelines decided to explore the castle since Madame had forbidden them to go outside. The first thing they wanted to explore was the tower. They followed its corkscrew steps to the very top. There they came to a barred door. What would they find when they opened it? A dwarf spinning straw into gold? A witch with a poisoned apple?

They were disappointed, because when they pulled the bolt and opened the door there was only an empty round room with tiny windows.

"Let's play Bluebeard," cried Brigitte. "I'll be Blue-beard's wife on the steps outside. Yvette, you be my sister Anne looking out of the window to see if my brothers are coming to rescue me. And the rest of you can just lie on the steps and be Bluebeard's murdered wives."

Of course all the orphelines understood the play without any more explanation. Yvette was to watch for the arrival of their brothers, the boy orphans.

Yvette went to a window and began her vigil. Brigitte banged on the door desperately. "Anne, Sister Anne," she cried, "dost thou see anyone coming?"

"I don't see anything but a lot of wet trees," answered
Sister Anne. "It's still raining, and I bet it will keep
on for forty days and we'll never get outside."

The murdered wives giggled.

Brigitte pounded on the door again. "Anne, Sister
Anne," she besought, "dost thou not see anyone coming? Hubert said they'd get here after supper."

"I wish they had come in time to eat with us," said
one of the murdered wives.

"Hush!" Brigitte reprimanded her. "You're dead and
can't talk."

But some of the wives grew tired of being dead.

16

"This is dull," complained Marie. "We can't see anything."

"And Marie keeps sticking her foot in my face," whined Charlotte.

"These steps are so hard," Lucette joined in. "We should get some pillows so we can be comfortable while we're dead."

But at that point there was a cry of triumph from the tower room.

"They're coming! They're coming!" cried Sister Anne. "There's an autobus coming down our road."

The murdered wives came to life completely and

went running down the steps to see the boys. But Brigitte opened the door and joined Yvette in the tower
room.

"I wish we could open these windows and lean out,"
said Yvette.

But they had to be content with flattening their faces
against the small panes and watching the autobus halt
by the bridge. It immediately exploded with boys. They
came flying from both ends of the bus. They gathered
in little groups, staring up at the castle while Monsieur
Roger, who was in charge of them, talked to the driver.

Brigitte began tapping the window panes to attract
their attention. Yvette waved wildly.

Soon one of the boys saw them because he was most
interested in the tower. The girls watched him turn to
some others. Soon all of the boys were looking up at
them. Both girls waved their welcome.

"Our knights," cried Brigitte. "Our knights have
come to rescue us from Bluebeard."

Two of the boys stooped and gathered something
into their hands. Then they threw the somethings at
the tower. There were soft ploppings below the window
and mud speckled the panes.

"How craven!" declared Brigitte indignantly. "Our
knights are throwing mud balls at us."

CHAPTER TWO

It seemed to the orphelines that they never would have a chance to get acquainted with the boys. Although they took their meals together in the dining hall, the boys sat at two long tables and the girls at their own.

Monsieur Roger sat at the head of one of the boys' tables. It was hard to think that he had ever been a boy himself. It was much easier to imagine him as a tiny man with a mustache who had popped out of a cabbage head and grown to full size.

He disapproved of talking at table and cast many a black look at the chattering orphelines. But he did not need to be so strict because the boys seemed to be interested in nothing but their food anyway.

And immediately after the meal was over, they were marched out of the dining hall to their wing of the castle.

Monsieur Roger privately told Madame Flattot the reason for his strictness.

"These boys should be in a reform school instead of an orphanage," he declared. "That Pierre came to us from the streets of Paris. Only yesterday he tried to set

19

Yvette put her arm around her shoulder. "Don't listen to him, Brigitte," she said. "You're a wicked boy," she told Pierre. "Some ogre cast a spell on you."

Pierre glanced at the small boy standing beside him. "Listen to these little goslings, Marcel," he said. He shoved the little boy toward the girls. "You can be their knight."

The little boy ran to Brigitte and made a clownish bow.

Josine immediately stepped behind him and gave him a shove that sent him sprawling in the dirt at Brigitte's feet. Marcel scrambled to his own feet and started for Josine. The littlest orpheline screamed as she ran for the safety of the castle, but she kept looking behind to see if Marcel was still following her. She stopped in the shelter of the doorway. "My knight has freckles all over his face," she taunted him, "and he can't catch *me*."

But Marcel had lost interest in her because he was needed by the other boys. Yvette had scraped out the hopscotch squares with the side of her shoe and Pierre was calling for help.

At his command the boys banded together and gathered rocks. They began throwing them at the girls.

Brigitte picked up a heavy clod and heaved it at Pierre. The other girls quickly followed her example.

22

When the jousting between the knights and their ladies was at its height, Monsieur Roger came hurrying down the lane.

"Stop!" he thundered, as a misdirected rock hit his ear. "Stop this scandal at once! Come here, you Pierre! Come here, all of you."

The boys sullenly shuffled toward him.

"They started it," accused Pierre. "We were just minding our own business and they came down here and started fighting us."

"We did not," declared Brigitte hotly. "We just came here and wanted to be friendly and play with them. They started it. They teased us."

"We did not," cried Marcel. "That littlest gosling pushed me into the dirt. She's an *enfant terrible*."

"Silence!" roared Monsieur Roger. "I have had enough. You boys go to the farm and help Hubert with the weeding. That is what you were supposed to be doing." He glared at the orphelines. "And you bold girls report to Madame Flattot immediately and tell her I have forbidden the boys to play with you."

The girls were very subdued as they returned to the castle. They told Madame Flattot their side of the trouble. They had asked the boys if they might play ciel with them, and the boys had immediately begun throw-

24

ing rocks at them. "And we didn't do anything at all to them," said Marie.

"I pushed Marcel into the dirt," admitted Josine proudly, "and he chased me. I think he's a handsome boy. His face looks like a big round cookie full of chocolate drops."

Madame Flattot listened to all the complaints then gave her judgment. "They are very wicked boys," she said, "and you are foolish girls. I forbid you to speak to them unless they improve."

Brigitte still smarted from Pierre's words. Were they true? She knew that they were really orphelines and not princesses. But did Madame and Genevieve pretend to love them only because they were paid for it?

"One of them said that you don't really love us," said Brigitte. "He said you just take care of us because you're paid for it. If Monsieur de Goupil stopped paying you, would you still take care of us for nothing?"

"That makes a real question," pondered Madame Flattot. "I could not live without an income. How would I pay my social security and buy my safety pins? No, I would have to go and work in a café in Paris."

The orphelines' faces dropped.

Madame gaily tossed her braid to and fro. "But, ah, there would be my day off every week," she continued.

"On that day I would go back to the café as usual. But I would not cook a soup or toss a salad. I would gather together all the eggs and sugar and chocolate I could find. Then I would bake a giant chocolate cake. I would bring that cake here, and one day a week we would be a happy family again and eat chocolate cake all day long."

The orphelines were pleased with Madame's answer. Of course she really loved them. Wouldn't she spend her day off with them instead of going to the cinema or a park in Paris?

But there was still Genevieve. If her pay stopped, would she be willing to bake them a chocolate cake once a week and spend the day with them?

They looked for her through the great rooms and stairways of the castle. At last they found her hanging the bedding out of the windows. The sheets looked like white banners flying from the castle walls.

They gathered around her anxiously. "Genevieve, do you really love us, or do you only take care of us because you are paid for it?" asked Brigitte.

"Suppose you didn't get any money for working here," put in Yvette. "Would you stay with us anyway?"

"Oh, là!" exclaimed Genevieve. "I could not work

26

free. My godmother wouldn't let me do that because she wouldn't think it was fair. I would have to marry that stupid Jacques she is saving for me." The orphelines groaned with disappointment, but Genevieve's face brightened. "But only on one condition," she went on. "That we adopt all of you and take you on our honeymoon. And after that, we would all live together on his farm in Normandy."

"And once a week Madame would come to visit us with her chocolate cake," finished Josine. "I hope she'll bake that cake even if she still gets paid for taking care of us."

So the girls were satisfied with the answers that Madame Flattot and Genevieve had given them, but they were disappointed in the conduct of their knights.

"And we'll never, never have anything more to do with them until they apologize," decided Brigitte.

"Can't I even push Marcel so he'll chase me?" pleaded Josine.

CHAPTER THREE

One morning when mists veiled the old castle in a dream, a most unchivalrous thing happened to Josine's cat, Swan.

The littlest orpheline often went to the barn to play with him and usually ended up by smuggling him into the castle. It was so easy to hide a cat in the many passage-ways and rooms. And Swan walked with such light *peti peta* steps that he often went unnoticed for many hours.

Then Madame would say, "Take the cat outside, Josine. No cats in the castle. Monsieur de Goupil has forbidden it. After all, Swan is not the Booted Cat so he cannot expect to live in a castle."

Monsieur de Goupil had been very nervous about the cats ever since the time that Swan had jumped from the window onto his shoulder when he was holding a teacup in his hand.

But this day Swan came to the castle of his own accord. He came flying in a white streak with a small tin pan tied to his tail. Josine found him by the back door, mewing sadly and sitting on the edge of the pan.

At first she thought that Madame had tied the pan to his tail, because it was one of the small light ones she didn't like for cooking. But Madame had been gone all morning.

Quick suspicion flashed into Josine's head. One of those boys had done it–probably Marcel. She would go and find out.

She loosened the pan from her cat's tail and took him into her arms. She started down the graveled road that led to the farm. Wait until she found that Marcel. Perhaps she would push him into the dirt twice.

Some of the boys were busy cleaning the fowlyard. When they saw her coming they gathered their heads together. Josine advanced upon them angrily, her eyes searching for Marcel.

"Somebody tied a pan on my cat's tail," she accused, "and I think I know who did it."

The boys immediately became sympathetic. "Poor cat," said Pierre. "It was that wicked ogre from the other side of the woods. You saw him do it, didn't you, Marcel?"

There was the little freckle-faced boy. He looked sufficiently frightened. "I ran away," he said. "I was afraid of that old ogre. He was tall as a church steeple and he had a fierce black beard."

Josine wasn't sure. "I think one of you did it," she maintained. "I think it was Marcel."

Pierre stepped up to Josine, indignantly tossing his bristly head. "And that isn't all," he said. "The wicked ogre has turned poor Madame Flattot into a hen. If you don't believe me, you can come and see for yourself."

Josine was worried. She went to the fence and looked through the wiring.

"It's that black and white hen with the chicks." Pierre pointed. "Madame tried to stop the ogre from tying the pan on the cat's tail, so he turned her into that hen. You saw it, Tintin."

"I told her to run," said Tintin, "but she wouldn't do it. Then the ogre tried to turn me into a dog." At these words a sudden spasm seized Tintin. He crouched down on all fours. "Ouaf, ouaf, ouaf," he began barking.

"*Hélas*, poor Tintin!" exclaimed Pierre. "You didn't get away fast enough. You're caught under part of his spell." He began to pat Tintin's head as the barking grew more ferocious. "Down, boy," he ordered. "Down, *toutou*."

But Josine wasn't interested in Tintin's plight. She was staring at the black and white hen surrounded by her yellow chicks. She did look something like Madame Flattot. She had the same bright eyes and plump figure. She even walked like Madame.

"Is it really you, Madame?" Josine questioned the hen.

Josine put the cat down. The partly bewitched boy immediately leaped at Swan with a fierce growl, and the cat dashed for safety.

Josine stood at the gate and watched the black and white hen. She was clucking fussily to her chicks. "*Glousse, glousse*," she clucked in Madame's anxious tone of voice. And when she cocked her red-combed head, gave Josine a sharp, bright look, and shook her

31

wings fretfully, the little girl was sure that it was Madame Flattot.

"Poor, poor Madame," she cried. "Perhaps Brigitte will know what to do about you."

She caught the hen and turned back to the castle. Tintin flopped after her on all fours, barking and snapping at the hem of her skirt. Josine gave him a kick. "Bad dog!" she said. "Why didn't you bite the wicked ogre?"

As she carried the hen in her arms she tried to comfort her. "Never mind, Madame," she said. "I will take care of you. When I was littler than you, you took care of me. Now that you're the littlest, I'll take care of you." She patted the hen and asked, "How does it feel to be a hen? Do the feathers stick you?"

But the hen made no answer.

Josine couldn't find anyone in the girls' side of the castle. Perhaps Genevieve had taken them to gather cabbages on the farm. Another fright came over her. Perhaps the ogre had turned them all into cabbages.

She would take Madame Flattot to her room and try to make her comfortable. She punched a nest into the soft comforter on Madame's bed and eased the hen into it. "You can rest now," she told her. "You won't have to cook or scrub anymore. I'll do it for you."

32

Then she jumped as a deep voice at the door demanded, "Josine, what is that hen doing on my bed?"

Behind her stood Madame Flattot without feathers or red comb. The little girl quickly looked back to the bed. There was the black and white hen. For a few seconds Josine wasn't sure which was Madame Flattot.

Then she realized that the boys had played a trick on her.

"I thought the hen was you," said Josine sheepishly. "The boys said a wicked ogre had turned you into a hen."

Madame Flattot was angry at the boys for the trick

they had played on Josine. She was angry with Josine for being so taken in. She was angriest at the black and white hen. She raised her skirts and shook them at her. "Shoo! Shoo!" she scolded. "Out of here, impostor!"

"I thought it was true," persisted Josine. "Everybody is always talking about princesses and ogres and fairies. Sometimes I don't know what is real and what isn't."

Madame Flattot closed the door on the hen's tail. "It has all gone too far," she declared. "There will be no more fairy tales. The business must end before we all lose our minds." She gave Josine a quick henlike glance. "And if an ogre ever changed me into anything," she ended, "it would not be a hen. It would be a formidable creature such as a rhinoceros or a tiger."

After the incident had been discussed by Madame, Genevieve and Monsieur Roger—to say nothing of all the orphelines—it was decided that the boys should either make a public apology to Josine or be kept in the castle for a week. They decided on the apology.

The littlest orpheline insisted on wearing her blue and white Sunday dress and her biggest hair bow for the important event. Genevieve even loaned her red necklace. All the other girls cast envious looks at Josine as she stood between Monsieur Roger and Madame Flattot in the courtyard.

The boys advanced in a group. They looked ashamed and self-conscious. They tried to make themselves small as they marched to Josine with bowed heads and lowered eyes. All but Marcel. He was grinning as happily as if he were arriving for a fête.

Pierre, as the eldest, stepped from the group and approached Josine. He nervously plucked at the blond quills of his hair.

"We, the boys of the orphanage," he began, "humbly beseech your—your—"

"Pardon," prompted Monsieur Roger.

The boy began again in a surer voice, "We, the boys of the orphanage, humbly beseech your pardon, Mademoiselle Josine, for the trick we—we—"

"Perpetrated," pronounced Monsieur for him.

"On you," went on the boy.

"And we will never let it happen again," added Monsieur Roger for himself as well as the boys.

"And I'm sorry I tied the pan on your cat's tail," added Marcel, although Josine did not think that he looked sorry at all.

"It was a scandal," declared Monsieur Roger.

Josine airily perked her hair ribbon with one hand

and twisted the red necklace with the other. Madame Flattot nudged her. Josine remembered her speech.

"I forgive you," she answered graciously, "because we are brothers and sisters in one big family."

"And we should live together in peace and love," Madame finished for her.

Then Pierre made a clumsy bow to Josine because he didn't know how to end the ceremony. Marcel pinched Tintin. The delegation turned and slowly marched away. But as soon as the boys reached the edge of the cobblestones they took to their heels as if an ogre were really after them.

Brigitte whispered to Yvette, "Weren't they knightly? Perhaps they will be that way from now on."

Monsieur Roger said to Madame, "The girls are as bad as the boys. Their heads are full of elves and butter-flies."

Madame Flattot felt guilty too. "Oh, I know that the forest of Fontainebleau has bewitched all of us," she admitted. "Perhaps we should take the children on a tour of the royal palace so they will become interested in real kings and queens. And I have always wanted to see Napoleon's rooms."

"It would be good for the boys too," Monsieur Roger agreed. "It will keep them from forgetting their history during vacation. I shall make arrangements with Hubert to use the farm trucks." He added severely, "We will keep the boys and girls in separate groups."

Madame turned to the girls. "And I forbid you to speak to the boys or have anything more to do with them until they have proven their good intentions," she commanded. "They didn't look too remorseful to me."

CHAPTER FOUR

Not all was play for the orphelines. They had many chores to keep them busy. They helped weed the farm gardens and gather in the vegetables.

One day they went with Genevieve to fill some sacks full of big onions which Madame planned to braid into garlands and hang in the tower room to dry.

Brigitte talked and dawdled so much that she was behind the others in her work.

"We will go back," said Genevieve, "and as soon as your bag is full, you may follow. Josine, perhaps you would like to stay to help Brigitte."

Josine agreed to stay, but she wasn't much help. She was trying her hand at braiding the onion tops, and Brigitte stopped pulling onions to show her how.

As they worked at the braiding Hubert's horse and cart came slowly down the road that cut through the field. Three of the boys were in the cart. It stopped near the girls. Hubert jumped out and started down the rows to take a look at the cabbages in the next field. The boys were left alone in the cart.

"Hé, if it isn't the little princesses braiding onion

tops," said Pierre. "Where are the others? At Prince Charmant's ball?"

Brigitte turned her nose into the air. "We can't talk to you," she informed him. "Madame forbade it."

"So the princesses can't talk," said Jean. "A witch must have their tongues."

Josine ran up to the horse. "We can talk to you," she told the heavy-hoofed beast. "Tell them that we are going to tour the palace of Fontainebleau sometime soon and if they are good, perhaps Madame will let us talk to them again."

"We're going too," said Pierre, "but we aren't going with you. Monsieur Roger said so. We are going to see Napoleon's hat and his sword."

Brigitte joined Josine. She addressed herself to the horse. "Tell those boys that the palace used to be a royal hunting castle long ago. I learned that in my history."

"We know that," retorted Pierre, "so we don't need a horse to tell us. And these woods were the royal hunting grounds."

Little Marcel spoke for the first time. "Maybe Hubert will take us rabbit hunting with him next fall," he said.

"May we go too?" asked Josine.

Brigitte warningly put her hand over Josine's mouth. "You can't talk to them," she reminded her. "You'll have to let the horse ask them."

"Of course you can't go," replied Jean, without waiting for the horse to repeat the question. "Girls can't go hunting."

Then Pierre leaned over the cart with a grin as wide as his face. "Maybe they would like to go on a cuckoo hunt," he suggested.

The other boys became enthusiastic at the idea. The girls abandoned the horse immediately because Madame had imposed silence on them only until the boys improved. That moment seemed to have arrived.

"How do you hunt cuckoos?" asked Brigitte. "Do you ride horses with hounds or shoot them with a gun?"

Pierre looked disgusted. "Maybe we shouldn't take them after all," he said, "because they're so stupid. You don't hunt cuckoos with guns or hounds," he informed Brigitte. "You have to get a big sack, like the one you have there, and go out in the woods. Someone has to hold the sack while we boys chase the cuckoos into it."

"Cuckoos are very shy birds," added Jean. "When they are chased, they fly into a dark hole to hide."

"I bet your Madame Flattot would make a wonderful cuckoo pie if we could catch enough of them," said Marcel. "I caught a sackful the first time the boys took me on a cuckoo hunt."

"I'll ask Madame if we may go," offered Brigitte eagerly.

"No, no," Pierre stopped her. "Why don't you make it a surprise? Think of how surprised she will be when we bring her a sack full of cuckoos for a pie."

"Why don't we go right now?" suggested Jean. "They have the sack and I heard some cuckoos calling in the woods beyond the barn."

Brigitte quickly emptied the onions from the sack while the boys hopped down from the cart. Hubert came back across the field, his wooden shoes stepping carefully between the rows of onions.

"We have to see Madame Flattot about something important," Pierre told him.

Brigitte was relieved. She really thought that they should ask Madame's permission to go hunting cuckoos. But as soon as Hubert had driven away, the boys began heading for the woods.

"Come on," they urged the girls. "Do you want the cuckoos to get away?"

"Shouldn't we tell Genevieve anyway?" asked Brigitte.

"No," refused Pierre. "If you tell her, all the other goslings will want to go. And such a crowd will scare the cuckoos away."

Brigitte said no more about it. She was happy that the boys were so friendly. They were really like brothers

42

now. Perhaps the time would come when they would be willing knights.

The children entered the mysterious forest. Great oak trees towered above them and hid the sky. It was very quiet and they could not hear any bird calls at all. They climbed over huge gray boulders sometimes, and at others their footsteps were deadened by the carpet of thick green moss.

At last the boys stopped in a thicket of pine trees.

"This is a good place," suggested Pierre. "We will chase the cuckoos here. They like pines."

He showed Brigitte how to hold the sack with its side resting on the ground and its mouth opened wide.

"Be sure to close it as soon as a cuckoo flies in," he explained. "And be very quiet. You'll have to be patient too."

The boys turned and went running through the woods. The girls waited expectantly. Brigitte kept adjusting the opening of the bag so it would look inviting to a cuckoo.

For a long time they waited patiently. Then Brigitte said, "My back's getting tired. Will you hold the sack for a while, Josine?"

The smaller girl took a turn at the sack, but her back tired more quickly than Brigitte's.

"When are the cuckoos going to come?" she whined.

"*Chut!*" warned Brigitte. "They will hear you."

More time passed. It was very, very still in the forest. The stillness was almost frightening.

"Perhaps they couldn't find any cuckoos," said Josine, and this time Brigitte didn't hush her.

"But I think we should wait for the boys to come back for us," she said uneasily. "It was so nice of them to take us on this hunt. We don't want them to think we are poor sports."

They waited a while longer.

Then Josine said, "I don't like cuckoo hunts. I want to go home."

Brigitte felt guilty at the thought of abandoning the hunt and disappointing the boys who had become so friendly. But Josine began to whimper, so Brigitte took her by the hand and started back through the woods. She hoped to come upon the boys and explain to them that Josine was such a little girl that she did not have much patience.

But there was no sign of the boys and every tree and rock seemed strange. They walked aimlessly, hoping to come upon some familiar landmark. Soon they reached a trail that led through leafy chestnut trees. But the trail was strange too.

At last Brigitte said, "We're lost in the woods like poor Little Thumb and his brothers."

"We should have brought some white pebbles and scattered them as we walked into the woods, like he did," said Josine. "Then we could find our way back."

"I wanted to bring pebbles," Brigitte began to imagine, "but I didn't have time. So I broke up bits of bread and dropped them along the way instead. But the birds have eaten them and now we can't find our way back."

"Perhaps we'll be lost all night," quavered Josine. "Perhaps we'll have to sleep under the leaves like Little Thumb and his brothers."

She began to gather leaves as she walked so she would have enough for a coverlet. There were floppy chestnut leaves like the feet of goblin geese, stubby oak leaves that seemed all thumbs, and clumps of pine needles to sew a witch's cape. One by one Josine dropped them into Brigitte's sack.

They heard something coming down the trail.

"The boys," cried Josine. "It's the boys coming after us."

But Brigitte quietly grabbed her by the hand and pulled her away from the trail. "It might be wolves," she whispered.

The two orphelines hid in the bushes. But it wasn't the boys or wolves. It was a dark man with a spade beard riding on a coal black horse. He had a riding whip in his hand, and a long-eared hound followed the horse's hoofs.

"The ghostly huntsman," whispered Brigitte. The girls crouched in the bushes like statues of cherubs in a palace garden. The specter passed on, although the dog gave an inquiring sniff toward the bushes.

Then Brigitte took Josine's hand and they left the trail for the open woods.

"We don't want to meet him again," said Brigitte.

They walked on and nothing looked familiar.

"I'm tired," whimpered Josine. "I don't want to be in the fairy tale anymore. I want to go home."

"We can't go home," said Brigitte. "We don't know where it is."

In a rocky gorge they came upon another trail, so they turned into it.

"It must go somewhere," said Brigitte.

As the gorge opened they came upon a strange sight. Ahead of them was a great cave where some figures were gathered around a campfire. Others were climbing the rocky cliff with the aid of ropes. They were in khaki shorts and had black neckerchiefs tied around their heads.

Brigitte's heart skipped. "The robbers' cave," she told Josine, "and those must be the robbers."

Josine began to wail. Brigitte didn't know whether to run or stand her ground when one of them came toward her. She then saw that he was only a big boy and that he had a friendly, sun-tanned face.

"What is wrong?" he asked. "Did the little girl hurt herself?"

"We're lost," quavered Brigitte. "We've been walking through the woods forever and we can't find our home."

A tall man in a green beret and khaki uniform like the boy's joined them. He had a friendly face, too, with smile wrinkles lightly drawn around his eyes and lips.

"Who hasn't done his good deed for the day?" he asked the boys. "What about you, Claude?"

"Please, *Chef*," the long-legged youth accepted, "let me take care of them. I'll take them to that old castle over the hill and ask the people there."

The girls silently followed the big boy. He led them back through the gorge and over a wild sandy waste. As they approached a grove of birch trees they heard the clopping of a horse's hoofs. The dark man came riding toward them.

Josine clutched Brigitte and Brigitte seized the boy's arm.

"The ghostly huntsman," she cried. "He is after us."

Claude looked at her with amusement. "It is only Monsieur Courcy," he said. "He is from Paris. He often comes out here to exercise his hunting dog."

Brigitte blushed with embarrassment at her mistake as the boy and the horseman saluted each other in passing. Then Claude continued, "Our troop is from Paris too, so we don't know much about this neighborhood. But the people in the castle should be able to help you."

They stepped from the birches into the sunlight of a clearing beside the road.

"If they don't know where you belong," said the boy, "you can wait there while they call the gendarmes."

They looked down the road. There was the old castle with its tower, donjon, and moat.

"That's our home," cried Brigitte joyfully. "We must have wandered around in a circle."

"People often do when they're lost," confirmed Claude. He raised his hand to his forehead in a salute. "At your service," he said.

But before they left him, Brigitte said, "There may be some boys looking for us in the woods. If they come to your cave, will you tell them that we are safely home? They must be worrying about us."

Claude waited to see that they reached the door of the castle before he turned away.

But when Brigitte told Madame Flattot about their adventure and their concern for the boys, she dashed their dreams.

"The boys are back here in the castle," she said. "You have been fooled by a very old trick. When I was a little girl in Provence, some of my schoolmates played it on me. Only they said we were going on a magpie hunt. They took me out in the cemetery and left me holding the sack while they ran home. But I can tell you that I was more patient than you two. Although night came, I still waited for them to chase a magpie into my sack."

"Weren't you frightened too?" asked Josine.

"If you think it was frightening in those woods," said Madame Flattot, "I can tell you it was worse in a dark cemetery among the tombs and cypress trees."

"But you gave up and went home at last, didn't you?" asked Brigitte.

"No," Madame proudly shook her head. "I did not go home until a searching party found me next morning."

Josine was impressed. "And if they hadn't found you," she said, "you would still be in the cemetery holding that sack."

Madame Flattot gravely nodded; then she frowned. "But those children were severely punished by their parents for the trick they played on me. And so shall it be for the boys. They will not be allowed to go on the tour of the palace."

Now that Brigitte realized the treachery of the boy orphans she was outraged.

"And we thought they had improved," she said. She turned to Josine. "It will take nothing less than magic to turn them into knights," she said. "*Strong* magic."

CHAPTER FIVE

When the truck brought the orphelines in sight of the royal palace of Fontainebleau, they were too overcome by its magnificence to speak for a few minutes. It looked so proud with its sharp roofs and stone walls yellowed by the ages. They entered a courtyard where a double stairway, shaped like a horseshoe, rose to the main entrance.

"It looks big enough for all the orphans in France to live in," decided Brigitte.

She was carrying a loaf of stale bread under her arm because they had been promised a visit to a carp pond where sightseers fed the fish.

Madame Flattot made arrangements for a guide to take them through. He was a square, weary-looking man with sleepy eyes and a droopy mustache. When he saw the group of children, he looked sad. But he bravely shrugged his shoulders, then fastened his eyes on them.

"You must not touch anything and do not crawl under the ropes," he commanded. "Keep together and do not dawdle in the rear." His voice then became businesslike. "To the right we have the wing of the White Queens and to the left the Chapel of—"

"When do we see Napoleon's rooms?" interrupted Madame Flattot.

"When do we feed our bread to the carp?" asked Brigitte.

The guide gave them a scolding look and began again. "To the right we have the rooms of the White Queens," he repeated.

They went from room to room and the guide kept on talking as if he were reading a history lesson.

Brigitte yawned and Josine stopped to make faces at herself in a great mirror. Yvette sat down to rest on a fragile gilt chair.

The guide went on and on with his talk, "Napoleon once said—stop breathing on that mirror, little girl. And do not sit on the chairs. It is forbidden."

Josine jumped back from the mirror and Yvette sprang from the chair as obediently as if Napoleon himself had given the orders.

The orphelines followed the guide on tiptoe over many slippery inlaid floors. They wished that the guide wasn't with them so they could go coasting on the soles of their shoes.

They were hushed by the splendor of the great

crystal chandeliers, magnificent tapestries, and marble statues.

"I feel like I have died and gone to heaven," Yvette whispered to Brigitte. "Look at that big marble fireplace."

"Did the White Queens ever cook supper in it for Napoleon?" asked Josine.

They went on from room to room, and like a prince exploring a strange castle in a fairy tale, each room they entered was grander than the one before.

Then Josine asked, "When do we get to the fish?"

And Madame asked, "When do we see Napoleon's rooms? I am very loyal to him."

"He lives with us too," Josine told the guide. "He's over one of our fireplaces. But we live in a poor palace."

The guide was disappointed with his group. "If you don't want to see the ballroom, we can go to Napoleon's rooms immediately," he offered.

"I want to see the ballroom," said Brigitte.

"I want to see Napoleon's rooms," said Yvette, "and his hat."

"I want to feed the carp," insisted Josine.

The guide clapped his hands briskly. "*Eh, bien*," he said, "since everyone agrees, we will go to Napoleon's rooms."

So they trooped through more halls and rooms and bumped into other groups of sightseers.

"Oh, là, it is getting crowded," said Madame Flattot. "We must surely keep together. This place is so vast that we may get lost."

Brigitte remembered the time that she and Josine had been lost in the forest. She thought about Little Thumb in the fairy tale. She began picking off bits of bread from the loaf and dropping them on the polished floors as they walked along.

In Napoleon's apartments Madame Flattot was so

overcome with emotion that tears glistened in her eyes. At sight of his bed with its rich hangings, she burst into tears.

As Madame mourned over the bed the guide told the history of several vases and statues, although the orphelines did not listen to him.

"But where is the famous court where Napoleon told his soldiers farewell before he went into exile on Elba?" asked Madame, because she wasn't interested in hearing about the vases or statues either. "I must see the court."

The guide gave her his weariest look. "Madame," he said patiently, "that was the courtyard where you entered."

"Then we must go back to it while I am still in the mood," insisted Madame.

As they turned to leave, her tear-stained eyes bulged with horror. The guide turned white as a widowed queen. They both stared at Josine holding a rare Egyptian vase in her hands.

"Don't startle her," warned Madame in a loud whisper. "Don't make any sudden movement. She might drop it." Then she began talking to Josine in a voice that was almost calm, as if she were addressing a sleepwalker on a roof. "Put the pretty vase back, dear," she coaxed. "Just raise your arms carefully and put it back."

Josine obediently set the vase back in place. "It's all right," she assured them. "There was nothing in it to spill."

The guide put his hand over his heart, then sternly said, "The children must leave the palace at once. I had a foreboding of this when I first laid eyes on them. I will take you to the Court of Farewells immediately."

So they didn't get to see all of the palace. But Madame was satisfied when she stood again at the head of the horseshoe stairway where Napoleon had told his soldiers farewell before he went into exile.

"Imagine the sight that day, Madame," the guide addressed himself to her. He pointed into the cobbled courtyard. "The carriage is waiting for him. His soldiers are lined up below. The drums are beating and everyone salutes as he descends the stairway."

The guide stepped down three stairs. He raised his uniform cap in the air. "Soldiers of my old Guard, I bid you farewell," he cried in a choked voice. He returned the cap to his head sideways, thrust his hand into his uniform jacket, and bowed his head in grief. It was such a touching scene that Madame Flattot burst into tears again.

But Josine asked, "When are we going to feed the fish?"

The guide became himself once more as he held out

57

his hand for a tip. He explained how they could go around the long wing and get to the carp pond. "And keep those children out of the palace," were his own words of farewell to Madame.

They had to follow the square, cobbled paths out of the courtyard and go around the wing to reach the pond, but it was worth it. There lay the smooth expanse of water like a giant palace mirror reflecting the glory of the yellowed walls and the tall green trees.

Other visitors were feeding the fish. Brigitte divided the loaf as fairly as she could, and the orphelines leaned over the stone parapets and flung crumbs to the carp. The gray fish streaked through the water and fought each other for the crumbs. Their big mouths opened and closed at the surface.

"I have heard that some of them are a hundred years old," Madame told the orphelines. "King François I had golden necklaces put on them."

The orphelines strained their eyes to catch the flash of a golden necklace, but these carp were quite unadorned.

When the bread was all gone, it took Madame some time to lure the girls away.

"Don't you want to visit the Garden of Diane?" she tempted them. "A lady says that it is just on the other side of that wing. We can rest on the grass."

With finger to lip, she led them to a doorway. She stepped inside and carefully looked up and down for any sign of the forbidding guide. Then she hurried them across the hall and through more rooms until they found a door on the other side.

The orphelines loved the garden with its sweeping lawns and curving paths. They feasted their eyes on the statue of the goddess Diane who was pulling an arrow from her quiver with one hand and resting the other on the antlers of a small deer.

"If we had some bows and arrows, we could fight the boys better," suggested Josine.

Madame Flattot was so tired that she spread herself generously over a stone bench and took off her shoes. The girls scattered to play and explore.

As Brigitte walked grandly across the grass, pretending that her fairy godmother had waved a wand and all of this great palace with its gardens belonged to her alone, she was surprised to see a familiar figure on one of the benches. It was the man whom the boys at the robbers' cave had called their chief.

She tripped over to him and made a regal curtsey. "Good day, Monsieur Chef," she greeted him politely. "Have you seen Napoleon's rooms?"

The man smiled and beckoned her to sit down beside

60

him. He was no longer wearing the khaki uniform but a trim dark suit.

"I hope you aren't lost again," he said. "You look like a pretty statue come to life in this garden. Have you been through the palace?"

There was something about his friendly manner that invited Brigitte's trust.

"We live in a castle too," she said. "We're really fairy princesses, but we disguise ourselves as orphelines."

The Chef's happy wrinkles deepened as he patted her hand understandingly. "Ah, yes," he said in a low voice, "one must be careful because grown-ups do not understand such things. Sometimes they even call it lying. Would you believe that I was once the Silver Knight of Burgundy and that I rode a white horse with blue and silver trappings? But I disguised myself as a little boy and my parents thought that my steed was a stick-horse."

Brigitte bubbled with laughter.

"Did you fight dragons?" she asked.

"I slew many, many dragons," he boasted, "and rescued many a fair maiden."

Brigitte's face sobered. "We want the boy orphans who live with us to be knights," she said, "but they

only tease us. They are very bad boys and weren't allowed to come on the tour with us today."

Then she told him about the cuckoo hunt in the woods and the evil spell which had changed Madame Flattot into a hen. "Do you have any boys?" she ended.

"More than I can count," answered the Chef. "You saw some of them at the camp."

"Are any of them as wicked as our boys?" asked Brigitte.

"No, indeed," said the man. "They are all knights of France. I know of a very strong magic that turns knavish boys into noble knights."

"And do they fight dragons?" asked Brigitte hesitantly, because she wasn't sure that they were still playing the fairy-tale game.

"Yes, we all fight dragons," he answered. "Of course the dragons today are much bigger than those of my childhood, and so many of them are invisible."

"Could you use the magic on our boys?" asked Brigitte eagerly.

"I have just that in mind," said her companion. "I am always looking for new boys. You say that you live in that old castle above the cave?"

"The castle is old, but we're new," said Brigitte. "We moved there in June, so our vacation started early."

63

The man rose slowly. "I must get back to my party," he said. "They will be waiting for me in the Gallery of François I."

Brigitte jumped up and he shook her hand.

"You'll really come and work your magic on our boys, won't you?" she asked anxiously.

"On the oath of the Silver Knight of Burgundy," he replied gravely. Then he gave her the same salute as the boy at the cave had used. He went up the path toward the place.

Brigitte hurried to find the other orphelines to tell them about her meeting with the Silver Knight of Burgundy who could slay dragons and work magic on bad boys. They were still discussing it as they walked back to the Court of Farewells where their truck would be waiting.

As the orphelines passed the horseshoe stairway they saw their guide lounging against the stone railing with a cigarette in his lips. They all waved to him and some of them called, "Farewell, Napoleon."

CHAPTER SIX

The orphelines were so excited about the magic that was going to turn the boys into knights that they expected the Silver Knight to arrive at their castle the very next day.

They took turns watching for him from the tower window between their chores.

"How will we know him?" asked Yvette. "What does he look like?"

Brigitte's eyes grew dreamy. "He will be wearing silver armor," she declared, "and he will be riding on a white steed with trappings of blue and silver."

So the girls eagerly awaited the arrival of the magical knight. Day after day they watched for him, but he did not come.

"Perhaps the dragon won the last fight," suggested Josine.

"Don't be foolish," said Brigitte. "The brave knights always conquer the dragons. Surely you've heard enough fairy tales to know that."

But the days passed and the orphelines talked less and less about the brave knight.

They had something new to talk about. Bastille Day was only a week away. That is the French Fourth of July and it falls on the fourteenth of that month. It is the day when the French Revolution began with the storming of the Bastille prison by the oppressed citizens.

"There will be speeches and fireworks in the village," said Madame Flattot, "and a wreath is to be laid at the statue of the soldier in the square."

The eyes of the orphelines sharpened with interest.

"Will we get to go?" asked Brigitte.

"Of course," answered Madame. "The mayor himself has asked for two orphans to lay the wreath. He wants a girl and a boy, so we have chosen Brigitte and Pierre. The others will march in the parade, so everyone will have a part."

But Pierre refused the great honor of laying the wreath.

"I won't lay a wreath with a girl," he flatly declared.

And if Pierre would not, neither would any other boy.

Monsieur Roger was so provoked that he spoke of dragging Pierre to the village in chains and handcuffing him to the wreath.

Madame Flattot did not believe in taking such extreme measures with children. "Perhaps Brigitte can

66

carry the wreath alone," she said, "and we can find some other patriotic task for Pierre and the boys."

But Pierre and the boys thought up their own way of celebrating Bastille Day.

The result was that Monsieur Roger came dashing into the great hall to see Madame Flattot. He was so angry that he was chewing his own teeth. In his hands were an old tin can, a greasy rag, and some firecrackers.

"I caught Pierre and some of the boys trying to make a bomb with these," he announced.

"A bomb!" exclaimed Madame Flattot. "Why were they trying to make a bomb?"

"To blow up the castle on Bastille Day," explained Monsieur Roger ominously.

Madame clutched at her heart with one hand and Genevieve's shoulder with the other.

"Mercy on us all!" she cried. "They are dangerous. I now see that it was a great mistake to combine the orphanages. I shall call Monsieur de Goupil and tell him that the boys must be taken back to their old building. And before Bastille Day."

But Madame Flattot did not get to call the head of the orphanage because the Silver Knight arrived at the castle before she could reach the telephone.

He must have been in disguise because he came on a dark motor scooter instead of a white horse, and he was wearing his khaki uniform instead of silver armor. But he brought magic with him.

The orphelines gathered silently in the upstairs hall while he was in conference with Monsieur Roger and Madame Flattot under the portrait of Napoleon. They must have talked long and earnestly because the waiting orphelines became very impatient. And when the talk was over, the Silver Knight did not leave immediately. He went with Monsieur Roger to meet the boys and talk to them too.

Madame Flattot's face was sunny when she joined the orphelines.

"That should fix our boys and keep them out of mischief," she said. "The visitor in uniform is a chef of the Scouts of France. He is going to start what he calls a wolf cub pack with them."

The girls were uncertain about this magic club.

"You mean they are going to pretend that they are wolf cubs instead of knights?" asked Brigitte with disappointment in her voice.

"Là, there is much more to it," said Madame. "They will be playing a story, but it is one written by an Englishman, Monsieur Rudyard Kipling. It is called THE JUNGLE BOOK, and it is full of animals who are noble. Another Englishman, Lord Baden-Powell, got this wolf cub idea from it. The Chef gave me a copy of the book, and Genevieve can read some of it to you tonight before you go to bed."

The orphelines were sure that they would not like Monsieur Kipling's book if there were no knights and ladies in it.

Genevieve was not enthusiastic either. "But I have seen the scouts hiking," she admitted, "and they looked very polite and healthy."

"You will learn more about them, Genevieve," said Madame Flattot meaningly.

The orphelines were always ready to hear a story, though. Evening found them listening intently while

Genevieve read to them from the book. Even Madame Flattot lent an ear as she sat darning stockings. Coucky toddled around the group, although he was too young to understand the story.

It was happening in far-off India. It was happening to a small boy named Mowgli who was lost in the jungle after his village had been attacked by Shere Khan, a ruthless tiger.

The orphelines forgot that they were not going to like the book. They gathered closer around Genevieve, and soon they were in the story themselves. Monsieur Kipling had not written it that way, but when the kind wolf mother found the boy, there were twenty orphe-

lines with him. They were safe too when she persuaded Akéla, the wise gray wolf, to allow her to raise Mowgli with her own cubs.

Genevieve skipped around in the book because she wanted to reach the most exciting parts before bedtime. She read about Baloo, the wise bear who taught Mowgli and the orphelines the law of the jungle. She read about Bagheera, the powerful black panther, who taught Mowgli and the orphelines to hunt and to protect themselves.

When she reached the most exciting place, even Madame Flattot felt as if she were in the story too. There was a big meeting at the council rock. The evil young wolves led by Shere Khan were planning to seize Mowgli and the orphelines and Madame Flattot. Would Akéla be able to save them now? Would Mowgli and the orphelines and Madame Flattot be devoured by Shere Khan? The wolves were snarling and howling for them.

Suddenly Genevieve, although she was too busy reading the book to be in it, raised her head in alarm. She could hear the howls too.

"What's that?" she cried, for the noise was coming closer and closer. There was no doubt about it now. They really were hearing bloodcurdling howls.

Genevieve snapped the book shut as if to drive the

wolves back into its pages. Still they could hear the frightening sounds in the courtyard.

"The wolves have come out of the forest," cried Genevieve.

Madame Flattot's face turned white. "They have surrounded us," she cried. "Where is Akéla?"

The howls grew louder. But Madame Flattot showed great presence of spirit. She flung the half-darned stocking into a chair. She ran to the heavy oak door. First she pulled the big bolt, then the little one. She turned the key in the lock. She dropped the latch. She hooked the chain.

Genevieve had presence of spirit too. She grabbed Madame's sewing scissors in her trembling hand and pointed them at the door.

"You shouldn't have read that story," whimpered Josine, because she believed that somehow the wolves had escaped from the book.

Then Coucky, who would not have known a wolf from a poodle, began to bawl with the fright he had caught from the others.

Josine clutched him protectively. "Don't cry," she tried to console him. "I will let the wolves eat me first." Then at such a noble thought, she began to cry too. "But I don't want the wolves to eat me either," she sobbed.

There was a battering of blows upon the door.

"Go away, bad wolves," ordered Madame Flattot bravely. "Go away or I shall call the gendarmes and they will come with their pistols."

"Open the door, please," shouted a voice that did not belong to a wolf.

"Please open the door," pleaded another voice.

Madame Flattot slowly relaxed. "It is only the boys," she said. "This was one of their tricks. I shall give them a good scolding."

But it was quite a while before she could talk to the boys. First she had to raise the latch. Then she had to turn the key. She pushed first the small bolt, then the big one. But she left the chain on until she had opened the door a crack and one of her eyes could see that it really was the boys.

"Good evening, Madame," Pierre greeted her. "We have been practicing our wolf howls so we can be tender paws in the wolf cub pack. Don't you think we are very good at it?"

Madame Flattot unhooked the chain.

"You are too good," she complimented them. "You have scared the girls to death and Coucky has had a crisis of the nerves."

Pierre slipped inside. He raised two fingers to his forehead in a wolf's ear salute.

"I come to ask for the honor of laying the wreath with Brigitte on Bastille Day," he said. Then because he did not wish to appear weak in resolution, he added, "I really don't want to, but I have to do a good deed today. It is getting late and I can't think of anything else."

"And why must you do a good deed if it is such a strain?" asked Madame.

"Wolf cubs have to do a good deed every day," explained Pierre. "That's what the Chef said. And if we don't get to be wolf cubs, we can't go on camping trips. I have never been on a camping trip."

"And we're going to take overnight hikes," said Jean.

"And explore the forest," said Tintin.

"And blaze trails through it," added Pierre. "That is why I want to be a wolf cub so very much."

"I am sure that Brigitte will be delighted to lay the wreath with you if it will help you to become a wolf cub," said Madame Flattot to Pierre.

Brigitte hesitated because she did not think that Pierre's invitation was much of a compliment. Then she politely answered, "I shall be very happy to lay the wreath with you, Pierre—and I really shall be."

Then the pack let out such air-splitting howls that Genevieve dropped the scissors she was still holding.

75

It gave Madame Flattot a start too, but she recovered quickly. She invited the boys in for cookies. All of them were eager to accept the invitation but Pierre. He shook his head warningly at them. "Thank you, Madame," he said, "but we cannot accept rewards for doing good deeds. That's what the Chef said, too."

"We're having a meeting in the barn," Pierre stated. "It's our jungle."

Then the wolf cubs turned away and went howling over the bridge toward the farm.

So the orphelines thought that there might be some good in the Scouts of France after all as they munched on the cookies that had been sacrificed by the boys.

Bastille Day was all they had hoped for. They dressed in their polka-dot dresses, and Madame Flattot put a new bunch of artificial flowers on her big hat. The mayor sent two autobuses, one for the girls and the other for the boys. The buses were festooned with the tricolor flags of France, and the drivers wore their old army uniforms.

The mayor himself greeted Brigitte and Pierre. He led them to a florist's van where the wreath was waiting. The wreath was enormous. It was made of red tulips, white carnations, and blue cornflowers. And from it flut-

tered a gold ribbon with the words Liberty, Equality, Brotherhood, which make the motto of France.

The beautiful wreath was braced between Pierre and Brigitte and their arms were arranged so the gold ribbon wouldn't be hidden. They raised their heads high. They were proud to be French. They were proud to pay homage to the soldier in the square. Even though his statue was rusted and the bayonet broken off his gun, he still represented all the men and women who had given their lives for France.

The parade formed, led by the mayor and a soldier carrying a big flag. They marched around the square once, then the wreath was laid at the base of the statue.

There was a minute of silence when everyone bowed his head in respect for the dead patriots. And it was natural that in this secret little minute the orphelines thought of their own parents who were now in heaven with the brave soldiers. They were thankful for good Madame Flattot, but no one can take the place of a real parent. Little Josine squeezed Madame's hand as they stood together because she had never known any other mother.

Then the band struck up *La Marseillaise*, the national anthem, and its strong notes went marching through the square, past the trees, and over the golden wheatfields beyond.

There were speeches and dancing in the streets, although the dancing wasn't supposed to commence until evening. Some people lighted firecrackers and threw them at their friends, but Madame Flattot did not approve of such imprudence.

"There will be a gala display of fireworks in the village tonight," she told the children, "and we can watch it from our upstairs windows."

"Won't we get to dance in the streets?" cried Brigitte.

"Do we have to go home now?" asked Yvette.

"We have shown our patriotism," said Madame, "and the bus drivers are waiting. It won't be a holiday for them until they have driven us back."

So back to the bus trooped the disappointed orphelines.

But the fireworks display that night made up for everything else at the fête which they had missed.

"Oh," breathed Brigitte as a deep boom in the distance was followed by a burst of red, green, and yellow sparks in the sky. "It is enchanted confetti."

"Ah!" gasped Yvette as a single flame of fire tossed into the blackness burst into hundreds of glittering lights. "It is the rainbow on fire."

79

"Hé!" cried Marie as a cascade of blue and green fires fell toward the earth. "It is a fiery fountain."

"Ho, ho!" cried Madame after the last bright lights had colored the sky. "It is time to go to bed and dream that you are dancing in the streets."

CHAPTER SEVEN

Despite Pierre's noble act, the girls were still jealous and unhappy about the JUNGLE BOOK story in which they had no part.

It was only for Genevieve that a part had been found.

"The Chef and I have been talking it over," Madame Flattot told her, "and we have decided that you are to be the *cheftaine* of the wolf cub pack."

The young girl looked suspicious. "What is that?" she asked.

"Ah, it is a very noble position," explained Madame. "Every pack must have a young girl in charge–a chiefess."

Genevieve looked gloomy. Like the boys, she felt that joining this club was going to call for sacrifices.

"Do I have to start fires and swim rivers and build monkey bridges?" she asked. "I have heard that scouts do such things."

"You shall do more than that," said Madame. "You shall inspire the boys and strengthen their characters and tell them stories and bake cookies for them. All over France are young girls helping boys to grow up right. Would you shirk your duty?"

"I don't know how to inspire boys," said Genevieve desperately. "I've always taken care of girls."

But Madame firmly pressed a booklet into her hands.

"It is the handbook of the wolf cubs," she said. "Take it to the meeting next Thursday afternoon and read it to yourself and them. It will inspire all of you."

"What meeting?" asked Genevieve.

"The meeting at the council rock in the jungle, of course," said Madame. "Where else would future wolf cubs meet? And you are to conduct it."

"I know where it is," put in Brigitte. "The boys have been meeting in the barn and we've been spying on them."

"They're making a wooden standard with a wolf on top of it," added Yvette. "It's the only thing about the club that is knightly."

So that was the way that Genevieve who feared wolves so greatly became the wise wolf Akéla and head of the wolf cub pack.

The orphelines didn't have much time to spy on the boys because their chores kept them busy. They helped with the housework, and some of the older girls even did the washing and ironing as well.

Charlotte was learning to cook, although she was not as devoted to the heavy iron pots as Madame Flattot.

She sometimes went down into the dusty wine cellar and cast envious eyes at the bright new pans that had been put away "until the iron ones wear out," as Madame Flattot had explained to Monsieur de Goupil.

One day it was the turn of Brigitte and Yvette to sweep the courtyard. They chased their brooms over the cobbles and pretended that they were poor Cinderellas having to drudge at the housework. It made the sweeping more fun and less work.

As they swept away Jean and Tintin slowly approached them.

"May we sweep the courtyard for you?" asked Tintin.

Brigitte raised her broom threateningly. "You go away," she retorted. "We've had enough of your tricks and you aren't going to run away with our brooms."

"We won't run away with them," promised Tintin.

As he put out his hand for the broom Brigitte clubbed his head with it. The blow upset Tintin's balance and he fell to his knees. He covered his head protectively with his hands.

"Please let me sweep for you," he begged on bended knees.

"If you dare move, I'll hit you again," threatened Brigitte, standing over her victim.

"But we really want to do it for you," insisted Jean.

He leaped at Yvette and grasped her broomstick. Yvette gripped it fiercely and a tug of war ensued. Back and forth they tugged each other across the cobbles. Yvette stumbled and fell. But she still clung to the broom.

Then Brigitte ran to Yvette's assistance and began battling Jean with her broom. Tintin got up and ran to help his companion. But as he did so, Brigitte tripped him with her broom and he went sprawling on the cobbles again.

As they fought the battle of the brooms Genevieve hurriedly came out of the door.

"Stop it!" she cried. "Stop this fighting. I am ashamed of you, Jean and Tintin. Have you forgotten your wolf cub honor?"

Jean let go of Yvette's broom and Tintin rose from the cobbles.

"We only wanted to do our good deeds for the day," said Jean in an injured voice, "and the girls won't let us. They started fighting us."

"We offered to sweep the cobbles for them," said Tintin, rubbing his bruised elbow. "There's nobody else to do good deeds for. If we lived in the village, we could help old ladies across the street and give directions to strangers. They wouldn't hit us with brooms."

Genevieve straightened the matter out.

"That is right, girls," she said. "The boys must do a good deed every day if they are to become full-fledged wolf cubs. It says so in the book."

Brigitte and Yvette reluctantly surrendered to the good deeds, but they held onto their authority over the brooms.

"You're not sweeping between the cobbles," Brigitte called Tintin's attention.

"You're raising such a cloud of dust it'll get those clothes on the line dirty again," complained Yvette to Jean.

When the boys had finished their good deeds and gone on their way, the girls swept the places they had missed.

Even Marcel did a good deed. He came running to Josine one morning with something clutched in his fist.

"Hold out your hand," he ordered the littlest orpheline, "and I'll give you a surprise."

Josine immediately clasped her hands behind her. She said, "I think you're going to drop a spider into my hand."

"No, I'm not," persisted Marcel. "Please hold out your hand."

Josine shook her head stubbornly. "I think you've got a bee in your hand," she said, "and you want it to sting me."

Marcel lost patience.

"If you don't hold out your hand," he threatened, "I'll drop it down your neck."

"If you do, I'll scream," said Josine, "and Monsieur Roger will come out and spank you."

"No, he won't," said Marcel.

"Yes, he will," insisted Josine.

"He won't."

"He will."

"Won't."

"Will," persisted Josine, and she was a stubborn child who was bound to have the last word with Marcel. "Will, will, will," she added for good measure.

At last Marcel had to spoil the surprise by showing her what he had. It was a fuzzy brown caterpillar with bright black eyes.

"I really want it for myself," he admitted, "but I'm giving it to you for my good deed."

Marcel put the caterpillar into her open hand. It began to crawl over her fingers.

"It's wonderful," said Josine, "and it tickles. But Genevieve said you aren't old enough to be a wolf cub."

Marcel longingly watched his caterpillar curl up in Josine's palm. "I will be in two years," he said, "and I'm beginning to get ready so I can be in Pierre's group."

Josine rose to the occasion. "Thank you very much for the caterpillar," she said, "and I think you have beautiful freckles."

Marcel blushed under the freckles. "And tomorrow I'll dig a long worm for you," he promised, "and when I'm a big wolf cub and go camping, I'll catch a fish for your cat."

Although the boys had a hard time thinking up good deeds, Pierre chanced upon the idea for one without searching.

He had gone down to the old wine cellar to look for a basket when he spied the bright new pans stacked on a shelf. He was sure that Madame Flattot did not know about them or she wouldn't be using those old black pots. As a pleasant suprise for her and a good deed in the bargain, he waited until she went shopping in the village.

Then he crept into the kitchen and began gathering the old pots together. It took several trips up and down the dark winding steps to make the exchange.

Pierre proudly arranged the new pans on the stove. Then he awaited Madame Flattot's return.

Madame was shocked at sight of the pans which she had discarded. "Now who has done this?" she demanded.

"I did, Madame," announced Pierre proudly. "And I carried all those old ones down. It is my good deed for today. Genevieve—I mean, Akéla—says that I am a born leader and that if I always do my good deeds, I may carry the standard when we hike."

"Pierre." Madame Flattot sighed. "It is like the good deed done by Vincent Bernos when I lived in Provence. A poor widow's roof fell in, partly destroying her house. So the people of the parish came to her aid. This Vincent Bernos gave up a day's work and pay to repair her electric wires. There was much talk about Vincent's good deed and do you know what came of it?" Pierre slowly shook his head. "He was arrested and fined twenty francs for wiring a house when he didn't have an electrician's license."

"But he was doing a good deed," protested Pierre.

"So he was," admitted Madame, "and I will have to say to you what the judge said to Vincent, 'I congratulate you upon your good deed, but I must condemn your lack of prudence.' "

Pierre's face clouded. "I thought it was a good deed," he said in a disappointed voice. "I want to be a chef in the Scouts of France when I grow up."

Madame gave him a second look. Then she seemed to

be straining to do a good deed herself. She patted the boy's shoulder.

"And so it is, Pierre," she said. "I am the one who lacks prudence. You may leave the new pans here. I really should learn to use them and not be so old-fashioned."

At last the girls had a chance to take part in the wolf cub pack's activities. It was only as audience at the boys' reception into the pack, but the girls were grateful for that. They felt like princesses getting ready for a court of honor.

"There will be a big campfire in the courtyard," said Madame Flattot, "and we shall see ceremonies and hear speeches. It will be a grand sound-and-light spectacle."

The boys did more good deeds by gathering wood for the fire. Marcel reverently helped set up the wolf standard, even though he was not old enough to enter the pack yet and could be only a spectator like the girls. He was so full of the spirit of service that he even offered to take care of Coucky during the event.

All of them carried benches to set around for the honored guests. The village priest was among them because he was the chaplain of the pack, and it was said that even in his long black skirt he could outrun and outjump any of the boys.

The Chef came on his scooter because he was to make the big speech. He brought badges and more booklets with him.

Genevieve cut a fine figure in her new blue uniform with the brass buttons and the perky beret. But someone had to knot her kerchief for her because she still tied her fingers into fancy knots.

The boys in their uniforms of navy blue shorts and berets with sky blue shirts formed a circle around her. Each yellow neckerchief was tied with two correct knots, one at the throat and the other in the ends.

One by one, they stood up and took the scout oath after they had asked the chaplain's blessing.

"I promise to do my best, to be faithful to God, France, my parents, the law of the pack and to render service to someone each day," were the words of the promise. And Pierre said his with the sincerity which had been lacking when he made his apology to Josine in the same courtyard. He said it without the reluctance he had admitted in laying the wreath with Brigitte.

At the word "parents," Madame Flattot's face glowed as brightly in the firelight as if it burned with

91

a flame of its own. And Monsieur Roger smiled benignly, which was not often his custom.

As each boy finished making his *promesse* his comrades gave out a great wolf howl, but no one was frightened by it tonight.

Brigitte leaned across the bench to the orphelines in front of her. "Why, they are taking the oath of chivalry," she said in an awed whisper. "They really are knights."

Then the Chef made his speech about the ideals of the Scouts of France. He reminded the boys that their motto was "Our best."

"You must think of others before yourselves," he said, "have open eyes and ears and always be neat, speak the truth and be cheerful."

Madame, as the mother of the new wolf cubs, had memorized her speech. She walked to Genevieve, carrying a bulky package under her arm.

She said, "Cheftaine, I have thought that this ceremony was a little like a scout baptism. So permit me to give this little package to all of you."

This little package was quite an enormous bag full of *dragées*, the candy-coated almonds that are so popular at French baptisms, and everyone present shared in the gift.

92

It was a date to remember along with Bastille Day, 18 Brumaire, which brought Napoleon into power, and that St. Médard's Day when the orphelines had first come to their castle with high hopes and noble fancies about their knights.

The new wolf cub pack came marching down the lane. Genevieve, in her chic uniform, was taking her little wolves on a hike to the palace of Fontainebleau—the outing they had once missed because of their naughtiness.

Pierre walked at the head of the column carrying the wolf standard because he was the leader. But there was a heavy worry on his heart. He hadn't done his good deed for the day yet. Perhaps he wouldn't find time because of this trip to the palace. He doubted that there would be any disabled soldiers to be helped up the stairs or any children to be rescued from the carp pond.

As the pack approached the old stone wall he could see all the orphelines sitting on it to watch the departure. There was sisterly pride in the girls' faces.

A sudden inspiration came to the boy. As he passed the girls he dipped the standard gallantly.

"At your service, princesses of the enchanted castle," he called out in a clear, strong voice.

He had done his good deed. He had brought pleasure to the romantic orphelines.

The girls squealed with joy. In a chorus they shouted, "Bravo! Bravo!"

94

Brigitte was so bubbly with pride and happiness that she squeezed Josine.

"Aren't our knights chivalrous?" she cried. "Now we shall live happily ever after."

95